Burglars, Ducks and Kissing Frogs
HUMOROUS SHORT STORIES

Contents

D1427535

PEARSON
Longman

Duck Boy © Jeremy Strong 2003
Kissy, Kissy © Louise Cooper 2003
Series editors: Martin Coles and Christine Hall

PEARSON EDUCATION LIMITED
Edinburgh Gate
Harlow
Essex CM20 2JE
England

www.longman.co.uk

The right of Norman Hunter, Jeremy Strong and Louise Cooper to be
identified as the authors of this work has been asserted by them in accordance
with the Copyright, Designs and Patents Act, 1988.

We are grateful to The Random House Group Limited for permission to
reproduce an extract from *The Incredible Adventures of Professor Branestawm*
by Norman Hunter published by Bodley Head.

First published 2003
ISBN 0582 79619 9

Illustrated by Lynne Chapman (PFD), Nick Diggory and
Simon Jacob (Sylvie Poggio)

Printed in Great Britain by Scotprint, Haddington

The publishers' policy is to use paper manufactured from sustainable forests.

Burglars
by Norman Hunter

Professor Branestawm rang the bell for his housekeeper, and then, remembering that he'd taken the bell away to invent a new kind of one, he went out into the kitchen to find her.

"Mrs Flittersnoop," he said, looking at her through his near-sighted glasses and holding the other four pairs, two in each hand, "put your things on and come to the pictures with me. There is a very instructive film on this evening; all about the home life of the Brussels sprout."

"Thank you kindly, sir," said Mrs Flittersnoop. "I've just got my ironing to finish, which won't take a minute, and I'll be ready." She didn't care a bent pen nib about the Brussels sprout picture, but she wanted to see the Mickey Mouse one.
So, while the Professor was putting on his boots and taking them off again because he had them on the wrong feet, and getting some money out of his

money box with a bit of wire, she finished off the ironing, put on her best bonnet, the blue one with the imitation strawberries on it, and off they went.

* * * * *

"Dear, dear," said the Professor when they got back from the pictures. "I don't remember leaving that window open, but I'm glad we did because I forgot my latchkey."

"Goodness gracious, a mussy me, oh deary deary!" cried Mrs Flittersnoop.

The room was all anyhow. The things were all nohow, and it was a sight enough to make a tidy housekeeper like Mrs Flittersnoop give notice at once. But she didn't do it. "The other rooms are the same,"

called the Professor from the top of the stairs. "Burglars have been."

And so they had. While the Professor and his housekeeper had been at the pictures thieves had broken in. They'd stolen the Professor's silver teapot that his auntie gave him, and the butter dish he was going to give his auntie, only he forgot. They'd taken the housekeeper's picture-postcard album with the views of Brighton in it, and the Professor's best eggcups that were never used, except on Sundays.

"This is all wrong," said the Professor, coming downstairs and running in and out of the rooms and keeping on finding more things that had gone. "I won't have it. I'm going to invent a burglar catcher; that's what I'm going to invent."

"We'd better get a policeman first," said Mrs Flittersnoop.

The Professor had just picked some things up and was wondering where they went. "I'll get a policeman," he said, putting them down again and stopping wondering. So he fetched a policeman, who brought another policeman, and they both went into the kitchen and had a cup of tea, while the Professor went into his inventory to invent his burglar catcher and Mrs Flittersnoop went to bed.

Next morning the Professor was still inventing.

It was lucky the burglars hadn't stolen his inventory, but they couldn't do that because it was too heavy to take away, being a shed sort of workshop, big enough to get inside. They couldn't even take any of the Professor's inventing tools, because the door was fastened with a special Professor lock that didn't open with a key at all but only when you squeezed some toothpaste into it and then blew through the keyhole. And, of course, the burglars didn't know about that. They never do know about things of that sort.

"How far have you got with the burglar catcher?" asked Mrs Flittersnoop presently, coming in with breakfast, which the Professor always had in his inventory when he was inventing.

"Not very far yet," he said. In fact, he'd only got as far as nailing two pieces of wood together and starting to think what to do next. So he stopped for a bit and had his breakfast.

Then he went on inventing day and night for ever so long.

"Come and see the burglar catcher," he said one day, and they both went into his study, where a funny-looking sort of thing was all fixed up by the window.

"Bless me!" said Mrs Flittersnoop. "It looks like

a mangle with a lot of arms."

"Yes," said the Professor, "it had to look like that because it was too difficult making it look like anything else. Now watch."

He brought out a bolster with his overcoat fastened round it and they went round outside the window.

"This is a dummy burglar," he explained, putting the bolster thing on the windowsill. "In he goes." He opened the window and pushed the dummy inside.

Immediately there were a lot of clicking and whirring noises and the mangle-looking thing

bolster: a large long pillow

twiddled its arms. The wheels began to go round
and things began to squeak and whizz. And the
window closed itself behind the dummy.

"It's working, it's working," cried the Professor,
dancing with joy and treading on three geraniums
in the flower bed.

Suddenly the clicking and whizzing stopped, a
trapdoor opened in the study floor and something
fell through it. Then a bell rang.

"That's the alarm," said the Professor, rushing
away. "It means the burglar thing's caught a
burglar."

He led the way down into the cellar, and there
on the cellar floor was the bolster with
the overcoat on. And it was all tied
up with ropes and wound
round with straps and
tapes so that it looked
like one of those mummy
things out of a
museum. You could
hardly see any bolster
or coat at all, it was
so tied up.

"Well I never,"
said Mrs
Flittersnoop.

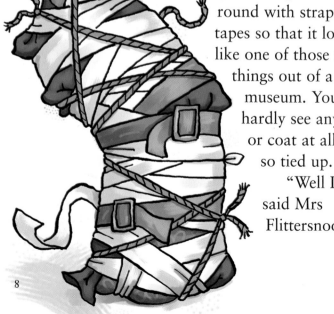

The Professor undid the bolster and put his overcoat on. Then he went upstairs and wound the burglar catcher up again, put on the housekeeper's bonnet by mistake and went to the pictures again. He wanted to see the Brussels sprout film once more, because he'd missed bits of it before through Mrs Flittersnoop keeping on talking to him about her sister Aggie and how she could never wash up a teacup without breaking the handle off.

Mrs Flittersnoop had finished all her housework and done some mending and got the Professor's supper by the time the pictures were over. But the Professor didn't come in. Quite a long time afterwards he didn't come in. She wondered where he could have got to.

"Forgotten where he lives, I'll be bound," she said. "I never did see such a forgetful man. I'd better get a policeman to look for him."

But just as she was going to do that, 'br-r-r-ring-ing-ing-g-g' went the Professor's burglar catcher.

"There now," cried Mrs Flittersnoop. "A burglar and all. And just when the Professor isn't here to see his machine thing catch him. Tut, tut."

She picked up the rolling pin and ran down
into the cellar. Yes, it was a burglar all right.
There he lay on the cellar floor all tied up
with rope and wound round with straps and
tapes and things till he looked like a mummy out
of a museum. And like the bolster dummy, he was
so tied up you could hardly see any of him.

"Ha," cried the housekeeper, "I'll teach you to
burgle, that I will," but she didn't teach him that
at all. She hit him on the head with the rolling
pin, just to make quite sure he shouldn't get away.
Then she ran out and got the policeman she was
going to fetch to look for the Professor. And the
policeman took the burglar away in a
wheelbarrow to the police station, all tied up and
hit on the head as he was. And the burglar went
very quietly. He couldn't do anything else.

But the Professor didn't come home. Not all
night he didn't come home. But the policeman had
caught the other burglars by now and got all the
Professor's and the housekeeper's things back,
except the postcards of Brighton, which the
burglars had sent to their friends. So they had
nothing to do but look for the Professor.

But they didn't find him. They hunted
everywhere. They looked under the seat at the

pictures, but all they found was Mrs Flittersnoop's bonnet with the imitation strawberries on it, which they took to the police station as evidence, if you know what that is. Anyhow, they took it whether you know or not.

"Where can he be?" said the housekeeper. "Oh! He is a careless man to go losing himself like that!"

Then when they'd hunted a lot more and still hadn't found the Professor, the Judge said it was time to try the new burglar they'd caught. So they put him in the prisoner's place in the court, and the court usher called out 'ush and everybody 'ushed.

"You are charged with being a burglar inside Professor Branestawm's house," said the Judge. "What do you mean by it?"

But the prisoner couldn't speak. He was too tied up and wound round to do more than wriggle.

"Ha," said the Judge, "nothing to say for yourself, and I should think not, too."

Then the policeman undid the ropes and unwound the straps and tapes and things. And there was such a lot of them that they filled the court up, and everyone was struggling about in long snaky sort of tapes and ropes and it was ever so long before they could get all sorted out again.

"Goodness gracious me!" cried Mrs Flittersnoop. "If it isn't the Professor!"

It was the Professor. There he was in the prisoner's place. It was he all the time, only nobody knew it because he was so wound up and hidden.

"What's all this?" said the Judge.

"Please, I'm Professor Branestawm," said the Professor, taking off all his five pairs of glasses, which fortunately hadn't been broken, and bowing to the court.

"Well," snapped the Judge. He was very cross because the mixed-up tangle of tapes and things had pulled his wig crooked and he felt silly. "What has that got to do with anything? Didn't you break into the Professor's house?"

"I left my key at home and got in through the window," said the Professor, "forgetting about the burglar catcher."

"That is neither here nor there," said the Judge, "nor anywhere at all for that matter, and it wouldn't make any difference if it was. You broke into the Professor's house. You can't deny it."

"No," said the Professor, "but it was my own house."

"All the more reason why you shouldn't break into it," said the Judge. "What's the front door for?"

"I forgot the key," said the Professor.

"Don't argue," said the Judge, and he held up Mrs Flittersnoop's bonnet that the Professor had worn by mistake and left under the seat at the pictures. "This bonnet, I understand, belongs to your housekeeper."

Mrs Flittersnoop got up and bowed. "Indeed it does, your Majesty," she said, thinking that was the right way to speak to a judge, "but the Professor's welcome to it, I'm sure, if he wants it."

"There you are," said the Judge, "she says 'he's

13

welcome to it if he
wants it'. That
means she didn't
give it to him,
did you?"

"No,"
said Mrs
Flittersnoop,
"I thought …"

"What you
thought isn't
evidence," snapped
the Judge.

"Well, what is
evidence, then?" said
Mrs Flittersnoop,
beginning to get cross. "I
never heard of the stuff. And I'm
tired of all this talk that I don't understand. Give
me my best bonnet and let me go. I've the dinner
to get."

"Oh, give the woman her bonnet," said the
Judge, and then he turned to the Professor. "If it
had been anybody else's house you'd broken
into," he said, "we'd have put you in prison."

"Of course," said the Professor, trying on all
his pairs of spectacles one after the other to see

which the Judge looked best through.

"And if it had been anyone else who'd broken into your house, we'd have put him in prison," said the Judge.

"Of course," said the Professor, deciding that the Judge looked best through his blue sunglasses because he couldn't see his face so well.

"But," thundered the Judge, getting all worked up, "as it was you who broke into the house and as it was your own house you broke into, we can only sentence you to be set free, and a fine waste of good time this trial has been."

At this everyone in the court cheered, for most of them knew the Professor and liked him and were glad everything was going to be all right. And the twelve jurymen cheered louder than anyone, although the Judge hadn't taken the least bit of notice of them and hadn't even asked them their verdict, which was very dislegal of him, if you see what I mean.

And as for Mrs Flittersnoop, she clapped her bonnet on the Professor's head, and then several people carried him shoulder-high out of the court and home, with the imitation strawberries in Mrs Flittersnoop's hat rattling away and the Professor bowing and smiling and looking through first one pair of glasses and then another.

Duck Boy
by Jeremy Strong

This story begins with a tragedy but ends happily. There! Now I've spoiled everything and told you the ending before I've properly begun. Then again, maybe I haven't, because it is really what happens in between the beginning and the end that makes this story so strange.

A mother was taking her baby son for a walk. She lived on the edge of a small town, and each afternoon she liked to walk beside the river. Her son James was just three months old. She would put James in his little pram and push him along the pathway beside the river.

The path followed the river for some way and eventually went right out into the countryside. The mother did not often go as far as that because, of course, she had to turn around and go home at some point. Besides, there was a bench where she always stopped. She would sit down and have a little rest before starting back home. The bench was on the top of a little hill, overlooking the river and the countryside. It was a wonderful viewpoint, and a good place to stop.

One day the mother stopped at the bench as usual. She parked the pram next to her and gazed around at the view. Maybe it was because the sun felt so soft and warm on her face. Maybe it was because the sound of the birds singing and the breeze rustling the leaves was so enchanting. Maybe it was because James was teething and his new teeth hurt and that had made him cry half the night and kept both of them awake.

Anyhow, the mother fell asleep.

James, however, did not fall asleep. He threw his rattle out of the pram. He threw his blanket out of the pram. He chucked out teddy and rabbit.

17

Now, by strange coincidence, just as James was chucking stuff out of his pram, a very untidy old lady was chucking stuff out of her kitchen. She lived on the edge of town and had just bought herself a new, red washing-up bowl. She flung the old one out of the window. It landed in the river and away it bobbed, out into the countryside.

By this time James had emptied his pram. There was nothing left to throw out so he made some very sloppy noises and filled his nappy. He was bored. Very bored.

All this time his mother slept on, dreaming of bluebirds and roses and champagne and knights in shining armour. The washing-up bowl bobbed nearer and nearer to where the pram stood.

James grabbed the sides of his pram and he began to shake it. He bounced up and down. He rocked violently from side to side. Then he shook the pram and bounced up and down and rocked violently from side to side all at the same time.

The pram rolled forward a little way. James rocked and shook and bounced, while his mother's head drooped lower and lower. The pram moved forward a little faster and then faster still as it reached the slope of the little hill.

And then, whoosh! Off went the pram, whizzing down the hill, while James laughed and gurgled and rocked and bounced.

And the washing-up bowl twirled and danced closer and closer.

Back on the bench his mother started to snore.

So it was that the mother was fast asleep when the pram finally reached the riverbank. It hit a fallen branch at full speed. The pram went head over tail and cartwheeled into the fast waters of the river. As for James, he was hurled from the pram, high into the air. Round and round he spun, laughing and gurgling, right out over the river. Then down he came, down, down, down until ... whump!

He landed in the washing-up bowl, which had reached that part of the river just at the right moment. What a stroke of luck!

The bowl, with James lying safely inside, went off down the river, gently bobbing up and down. He dabbled his fingers in the water and laughed and gurgled when the little fish tickled his fingers. He gazed at the ducks and geese and swans and thought them very beautiful. At last he became too tired to do anything except sleep.

Back on the bench, the mother woke up. Oh horror! Imagine the terrible scene! She was tearing out her hair and wailing away. "Where's my son?" Then she saw the pram in the river, caught against the far bank. It was empty. The mother could hardly bear to breathe any longer. Her son was dead, and it was all her fault.

Of course, you and I know it wasn't all her fault because James had done an awful lot of bouncing and rocking and so on. Nevertheless, if the mother had stayed awake she would have been able to prevent the tragedy from ever happening. But she hadn't stayed awake, and it had happened. She was heartbroken.

But you are probably wondering what happened to little James. The washing-up bowl carried him a long way from the town. He went on down the river until nightfall, when the bowl was caught in some overhanging tree branches near the riverbank. And there it stayed until morning, when James woke up and began to cry. He was hungry. His teeth hurt. His nappy needed changing.

* * * * *

James' cries were heard by a family of ducks, and Mother and Father Duck swam over to investigate.

"A baby human!" said Father Duck.

"All on its own!" said Mother Duck. "We had better look after it."

They grabbed the washing-up bowl with their beaks and between them they pulled it across to their nest. They pushed and heaved and shoved until they got that bowl out of the water and into the nest. The five ducklings in the nest were not

terribly pleased to find themselves sharing their bed with a washing-up bowl full of three-month-old baby and a stinky nappy.

However, the parents explained that the baby needed their help. "When a human finds a duckling all on its own they pick it up and look after it, so we are doing the same thing, but the other way round. This baby needs a home and parents and brothers and sisters just as you do. We shall all help look after it."

That is exactly what they did. James was well cared for in the ducks' nest. They fed him with waterweed and little snails and all things green and gloopy. They changed his nappy and washed him in the river. They told him bedtime stories about the great duck heroes of the past – Donald, Jemima and Daffy. In fact, they treated him just like their own little ducklings.

The days he spent with the duck family turned into weeks. The weeks became months and then years.

James learned everything from the ducks. His first word was 'Quack!' In fact his second word

was 'Quack!' too, and so were the third and fourth, but at least the ducks knew what he was talking about.

They taught him how to swim, and in fact James paddled before he could walk. He became very good at swimming. The duck family taught James duck-paddle of course, but James could do something else that was quite new to the ducks. He could do front crawl with his arms, and what with this technique and duck-paddle he was much faster than the ducks.

"That is brilliant!" cried Father Duck. "How do you do that?"

So James taught the duck family how to do front crawl. The ducks found it very difficult at first because they were not used to making one wing do something different from the other wing. They went round in frantic circles, splashing everyone and everything. They ploughed underwater and almost drowned. But bit by bit the ducks learned how to do front crawl with their wings, and then they became the fastest ducks on the river. In fact, they were the fastest ducks ever.

James taught them backstroke too, and the duck family could often be seen out with James, lazily swimming upstream on their backs and sunning their bellies.

Ducks from miles around would come and watch in astonishment as James and his foster parents went whizzing up and down at such speed that they made huge waves on either side of the river. Word of their achievements began to spread even further afield and soon ducks and swans and geese were flying in from all over the country.

They wanted to know how it was done. James began teaching front crawl to all the water birds and soon the sky was filled with birds arriving to join his swimming classes. One clever bird soon realised that if she could swim faster by doing front crawl then perhaps it would help her fly faster, too. She tried it out and it did. She could fly three times faster than before! On her back, too!

James had shown the ducks a new future and it was rapidly turning into the latest craze. It was not long before the skies were full of birds rocketing past at hyper-speed. As for the river – it was as if all the ducks had turned into mini powerboats.

Obviously it would not be long before
people began to notice.

A large party of hunters trooped down to the
river one evening to do some duck shooting. First
of all they were astonished to see so many birds
and so many different kinds of bird. Usually the
hunters had to hide in the bushes and make
duck-type noises to attract their victims. But now
they didn't need to bother. There were ducks
everywhere – great flapping piles of them! The
ducks were so busy looping the loop and stunt
flying, they didn't even notice the hunters.

The hunters thought that shooting the ducks
was going to be a doddle and they began banging
away with their guns. What a surprise they got!
Those birds were faster than bullets!
They went whooshing right past
the hunters. They went
whizzing up into the sky
like rockets.
They were like
express trains
charging through
the sky, one after

the other. There were so many of them and they were so fast the hunters got dizzy and fell over in a heap in the water. They trudged off home, soaking wet, without a single dead duck.

The ducks themselves were delighted with the way things had turned out. They felt that James had saved their lives. However, James pointed out that if the ducks had not looked after him when he arrived in the washing-up bowl he would not be alive himself.

All in all everyone was very happy – all except for James' mother. Three years had now passed since his disappearance and she had never got over that terrible day. She had just about shut herself indoors ever since and spent most of the day sitting in a chair and staring dully at the television. Sometimes she switched it on.

The hunters were rather disappointed that they had been unable to bag a single duck. However, they could not stop talking to each other about how those ducks had escaped.

"Did you see how fast they could fly? It was almost as if they were swimming through the sky!"

"I saw one doing backstroke!"

"And one looked like a baby boy. Strange. Very strange."

The hunters told their friends. The friends told their friends. More and more people heard about the speeding ducks. More and more people went down to the river to watch them. It was, after all, an extraordinary sight. It is not every day that you see ducks thundering up and down a river so fast that they leave huge, foaming bow waves, just as if they are powerboats. Nor is it every day that you can look up into the sky and see ducks looping the loop and performing barrel rolls like an aerobatics display team.

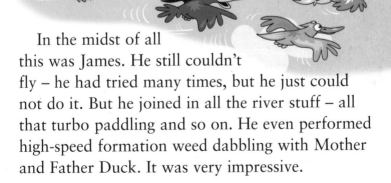

In the midst of all this was James. He still couldn't fly – he had tried many times, but he just could not do it. But he joined in all the river stuff – all that turbo paddling and so on. He even performed high-speed formation weed dabbling with Mother and Father Duck. It was very impressive.

The newspapers and TV shows got to hear about it. One day James woke up to discover that he could barely see the other bank of the river – it was completely covered with camera crews and newspaper journalists. Flash bulbs popped and cameras whirred.

The main news that night was full of the story of the amazing ducks and Duck Boy. (In other words, James.)

"It's true," said the newscaster. "It is just like the story of Tarzan, the boy who was brought up by apes. But this little baby was abandoned by the river and he was taken in and raised by a family of ducks. The local hunters call him Duck Boy."

It just so happened that on this particular day James' real mother had decided to switch on her television. Her mouth fell open and her jaw

dropped lower and lower. Could it be? Could it?

The boy looked just like James. He was bigger of course, but he had the same blue eyes, the same smile. Her heart began to beat faster and faster. She could hardly bear it. She couldn't tell if she was excited or scared or sad or happy or worried or maybe all of them together.

She leaped from her chair and hurried down to the river. It was the first time she had been back since the terrible accident. Her heart was thundering and her brain was asking the same question over and over again. Is it really James?

But when she reached the river great crowds lined the banks and she couldn't see. She pushed forward until she broke through the crowd by the water's edge and she stared across, hardly daring to look, her heart full of hope.

And then she saw James. He was older and bigger and dirtier but it was definitely James. She knew at once, in the way that mothers do know such things. Before she even knew what she was doing she waded into the water and started to make her way towards him. She held out her arms to her son and called.

"James! James! It's me – your mother!"

James splashed and stopped doing synchronised swimming with his duckling brothers and sisters.

There was something familiar about the human's voice that called him. He watched the woman wading towards him.

"James! It's me!"

"Quack?" said James, because of course he could only speak Duck.

James' mother stopped dead. Quack? Was that the way to greet your long lost mother? For a moment she was angry and then she realised, in the way mothers realise such things, that of course James would have learned to speak Duck. So she answered him like this: "Quack!"

"Quack!" cried James excitedly.

"Quack, quack!" shouted James's mother, pushing towards him even faster.

"Quack, QUACK! QUACK!" yelled James. They understood each other perfectly! It was incredible.

So it all ended
happily after all.
What a story!
There was only
one thing left to
decide, and that
was … would
James go back to
land and live
with his real
mum, or would
his real mum get
into the river,
learn to swim
and be a duck?
What do you think?
I can tell you
that James himself
became the greatest Olympic swimmer on Earth,
even though he had a rather unusual style. He
found it impossible to swim without quacking an
awful lot, and very loudly. Olympic swimming
events were incredibly noisy for many years.

* * * * *

The moral of this story is: be kind to ducks;
you never know when you might need their help.

Kissy, Kissy
by Louise Cooper

Gogglina the frog had lived in the palace garden pond since she was a tadpole. She reckoned it was pretty okay. There were lots of lily pads to jump around on, and loads of flies and slugs and other lovely things to eat. And Grandma Glugga, who ruled the pond, said it had the best, softest, squelchiest mud in the whole kingdom.

Grandma Glugga spent most of her time in the squelchy mud. She didn't know the half of what Gogglina and her friends got up to. She didn't see them when they sprang out of the pond to scare passing princesses, who ran away screaming and waving their arms around. She didn't notice when, at the evening croak-ins, they sang rude words to all the old songs.

And she didn't notice the Prince.

Gogglina did, though. He wasn't one of the usual princes, and he didn't do the things princes normally did, like play football or gallop around on a horse shouting 'Yo!' Instead, he sat near the edge of the pond, *sighing*. Gogglina was puzzled. Princesses sighed a lot, but they were soppy and romantic. Princes should be different. This prince was gloomy, too. In fact, he positively gloomed wherever he went. Something was obviously wrong. And soon, Gogglina's curiosity got the better of her.

Frogs weren't supposed to talk to humans. In fact, humans weren't supposed to know that frogs *could* talk. But Gogglina couldn't resist. One morning, as the Prince sat glooming as usual, she hopped onto a lily leaf and said (because frogs aren't very tactful):

"Hello! Why are you such a misery guts?"

She expected the Prince to yell in surprise and wave his arms around. But instead his face lit up with joy and he cried, "You recognise me!"

"Eh?" croaked Gogglina, baffled. "Recognise you? 'Course I don't! What are you on about?"

"I'm not a prince!" cried the Prince. "I'm a frog, just like you!"

"*Eh?*" said Gogglina again.

The Prince knelt down at the edge of the pond so that he could talk to Gogglina properly. "I was turned into a prince by a horrible, wicked witch," he told her. "It was really unfair; I mean, I didn't *know* it was her pet wasp when I ate it! But she put a spell on me, and now I'm ... *this*!" He shuddered.

"Wow!" said Gogglina. "How *revolting*! Poor you!"

"That's why I'm so miserable," said the Prince – or frog. "There's only one way to undo the spell, you see. I've got to be kissed by a girl frog." He gazed at her longingly. "*You're* the most beautiful girl frog I've ever seen."

"Am I?" said Gogglina, going all wriggly inside. "Really?"

"Oh, yes!" declared the Prince. "You're *gorgeous*. Will you give me a great big smacking kiss and turn me into myself again? Oh, please!"

Gogglina didn't know what to do. Okay, she was sorry for the Prince – or frog. Who wouldn't be? But the idea of *kissing* him ... that was truly *gross!* All that horrible pink skin, without a trace of proper green; and that creepy-crawly hair stuff on his head … And the things that humans ate: *cake* and *peanut butter* and *ice cream* … *Yuk!* It made her feel sick just to think about it!

"Please!" begged the Prince again. He puckered his mouth and shut his eyes. "Just one! That's all it needs. And you're *so* beautiful …"

Gogglina did feel sorry for him; she really did. But –

"No *way!*" she croaked in horror. And she took a flying leap off the lily pad, and dived to the bottom of the pond to find Grandma Glugga.

* * * * *

"Wicked witch, pooey!" Grandma Glugga snorted. "I don't believe a word of it. Even the wickedest witch in the world wouldn't be *that* cruel. If you ask me, that story is a load of old

snail slime. He's a nasty human, and he's trying to
fool you. Of *course* he wants a kiss from a girl
frog. They all do, you know. Think what it must
be like to have to kiss a crawly, pink princess –
urrgh! But he doesn't fool me. If he claims to be a
frog, he's got to prove it."

"How, Grandma?" said Gogglina.

"By doing the things every self-respecting frog
can do, of course. For instance, how far can he
jump?"

"I didn't ask," said Gogglina.

"More fool you, then. Can he catch and eat
umpteen flies in one minute? If he can't, then he's
no better than he should be and ought to do
somersaults." (Grandma Glugga had lots of
favourite sayings, and most of them didn't make
much sense.) "Can he croak the latest songs? Can
he croak *at all?*"

"I don't know," said Gogglina, and blinked,
feeling silly.

"Well then. Standing on your head doesn't get the spawn pickled, does it?" Grandma heaved herself out of the mud with a loud sucking noise. "I'll have a word with this prince. Because no grand-tadpole of mine's going to make herself ill by kissing a *human* unless there's a reason as tasty as cabbage white butterflies!"

* * * * *

The Prince was blubbing by the side of the pond when Gogglina and Grandma Glugga popped their heads above the water. Grandma snorted, "Cry-baby! He ought to have his nobbles gurgled!" But when he saw them he cheered up.

"I can prove I'm a frog!" he said. "I never boast, but in my proper shape I could jump straight across this pond from one side to the other! And I could eat *squillions* of flies a minute. And croak any hit song you care to name!"

"Hmmph!" said Grandma Glugga. "You never boast, eh? Well, we'll soon see how much webbing's between *your* feet! Because you're going to have to do it in human shape, aren't you?"

The Prince's face fell. "Don't I get the kiss first?" he asked.

"Not while I've still got blobs on my grummet!"

said Grandma. "Come on, my lad – it's test time. And unless you get top marks, then you can turn round and go right back where you hatched from, or I'm a frizzling fruit fly!"

* * * * *

Word soon got round, and by the time the Prince's test began, every frog in the pond had gathered to watch.

The Prince – who said that his proper, frog name was Golp – crouched at the edge of the pond. Grandma Glugga was on the far side, and Gogglina squatted next to her.

"Right!" shouted Grandma. "First test – lily pad jumping. On your marks!"

The Prince drew a deep breath, puffing his chest out. Some of the frogs round the pond sniggered.

"Get set!" bawled Grandma.

The Prince stuck his elbows out and shut his eyes. The sniggers were louder.

"GO!" bellowed Grandma.

And this is what they heard:

"Yeee-HAAA!" That was the Prince.

Sproing! That was the Prince jumping.

Wheee ... That was the noise of him flying through the air.

WALLOP! That was the sound of him landing on the lily pad. So far, so good.

Then:

Splob. That was the lily pad tipping over under the Prince's weight. The Prince said something like, "Ooh-er ... yipes ... WAAAH ..."

And the next noises went like this:

"*Aaarrgh!*"

Ker-SPLOSH!

"*Guggle ... globble ... urrrk ... glug-glug-glug ...*"

SKWUDGE.

For a few moments there was complete silence. Then the croaking began, as the frogs laughed themselves sick. A passing princess screamed and ran away, waving her arms around, but the frogs took no notice. They clutched each other, rolling on their backs and kicking their legs in the air.

Several of the youngest ones laughed so much
that they gave themselves hiccups and had to be
taken away for a nice mouthful of mud to calm
them down.

The Prince had had several mouthfuls of mud.
He was spitting out black blobs of it as
he struggled up from the depths
of the pond. He looked like a
black blob
himself, so
completely
plastered in the
soft, squelchy
stuff that you
couldn't even
tell which side
his face was.
The frogs
hooted more
than ever, until Grandma Glugga's voice
bellowed over the din. "That's enough! Ponk me
for a slug-sniggler, I've never heard the like! SHUT
UP!"

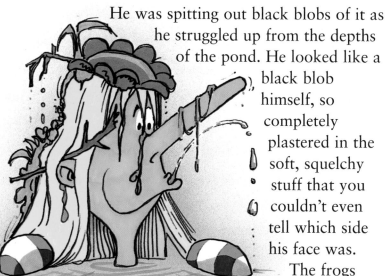

"PTOO!" The Prince spat out more mud, and
two sad eyes looked out from his slimy face.
"How did I do?" he asked pathetically.

"Middling," said Grandma. "But I suppose

that's better than a flink on a dropsical daddy longlegs." She blinked impatiently. "Come on, come on! I know it's lovely mud, but you can't sit around in it all day. You've got work to do. Time for your next test."

"Er ... which one's that?" asked the Prince nervously.

Grandma grinned across the whole width of her face, in the way that only frogs can.

"*Flies,*" she said with relish.

* * * * *

Bzzzz ...
SNAP!

Zee-owww! The fly zipped away, and the Prince sat rubbing his jaw. "Ow," he said. "That *hurt.*"

"Stuff and newt-sense!" Grandma Glugga scoffed. "Any *real* frog knows you're supposed to use your tongue!" She eyed a passing gnat, then her own tongue went *flick.* The gnat never knew a thing about it.

"But my tongue isn't long enough!" the Prince wailed. He gazed longingly at Gogglina. "You really *are* beautiful. Can't I have the kiss now? *Please?*"

"Certainly not, or I'm a fandangled

puddleduck!" snorted Grandma. "Come on! Your total so far is one housefly, two greenflies, half a bumble-bee – it got away but we'll call it half – and a maybug that should have known better. I don't call *that* very impressive!"

"But they taste horrible," moaned the Prince. "They make me feel sick."

"What?" Grandma was outraged. "Crumple my facets, I never thought I'd live to hear a frog say such a thing about delicious flies!" She eyed the Prince suspiciously. "I think you're *definitely* not a frog at all."

"I am, I am!" the Prince wailed. "It's only because I've got a human body that I don't like eating flies! If I was in my proper shape, I'd *love* them!"

"He is greener than he was, Grandma," said Gogglina. "Look at his face."

"We-ell ... I suppose he *is* a bit more frog-coloured," Grandma Glugga admitted grudgingly. "All right then. Try again. Bluebottles, greenbottles, purplebottles-with-pink-stripes, bees, fleas, anything with wings, anything that stings –"

"I don't want to get stung!" wailed the Prince.

"Oh, stop being a weedy-globber and get on with it!" said Grandma.

* * * * *

The Prince managed to swallow twenty-three assorted flying insects before he had to run away and be sick. Grandma Glugga admitted that now he really *had* turned a nice shade of green. His eyes were starting to bulge, too. Very encouraging.

"Right," she said, when the Prince tottered back. "One last test."

The Prince gazed yearningly at Gogglina. "Can't I have –"

"No!" Grandma interrupted sternly. "Song time first. Start with the one that goes: *Rrrrrak-rrak-ribbit, kek, kek, kek!*"

"I know it!" cried the Prince, and started to sing. "*Ooo, baby, ya really got me hoppin'* –"

"Don't *human* it!" Grandma was outraged. "*Croak* it!"

"Oh." The Prince's face fell. "It won't be as good as my frog voice. If I could only have –"

"GET ON WITH IT!" bawled Grandma.

The Prince sighed. "All right." He looked longingly at Gogglina again. "I'll sing it especially for you. It's a *love* song."

Gogglina blushed, which for a frog means turning a darker shade of green. And the Prince started to croak.

"*Ker-er-er … cakcakcak, cakcakcak; trrrriddle-iddle, gollup. Krakra-krak, urg, urg, gollup, gollup, gra-a-a-arr …*"

It was the saddest, soppiest love song in the frog charts. And the Prince did it beautifully. All the girl frogs started to sigh, and even some of the older ones gulped. As for Gogglina, she just sat there, totally besotted.

"*Ka-raaaa … ka-raaaa … gollup, gollup … GLUMMMM!*" The Prince finished on an utterly heart-rending croak that could be heard inside the palace.

For a moment there was silence. Then, all around the pond, dozens of girl frogs started to scream and pretend to faint.

Gogglina said, "*Wow …*"

The Prince blinked, swallowed, and asked in a small voice, "What do you think?"

Grandma Glugga stared at him. Then a single, big, fat tear rolled down her cheek and went *splot* into the pond.

"Well, croodle my nubkins," she said. "He *is* a frog!" She turned to Gogglina. "Go on, girl, what are you waiting for? Time wasted is time bewiggled! Kiss him!"

Gogglina went slowly towards the Prince. The Prince bent down. Gogglina looked up. The Prince puckered his mouth and shut his eyes blissfully.

Sssssss … MACK!

There was a greeny-yellow flash and a sort of muffled *bang*. When the smoke cleared, the Prince had vanished.

In his place was a drop-dead-gorgeous boy frog.

Gogglina said, "*Wow!*" again. She beamed at the Prince (we'd better call him Golp now) and gave a little wriggle, right down to her toes. "*Brill!*" she added.

Golp grinned at her. "Hey," he said, "that is *better*! Thanks, babe – I owe you one!"

He started to hop away. Gogglina's face fell. "Wait a minute!" she said, "Where are you going?"

"Uh?" Golp looked surprised. "Home, of course! To my girlfriend."

"Girlfriend?" Gogglina was horrified. "What about me?"

Golp laughed. "Look, you've done me a *big* favour, sure you have. Really appreciate it, and all that. But you're just a kid, right? My Glub's a *proper* girl!"

"Then why didn't *she* kiss you and turn you back?" wailed Gogglina.

"What? Kiss a *human*?" said Golp. "Get real, babe! Be seeing ya!"

And he leaped, *sproing*, from the pond and away across the palace garden.

All the frogs looked at poor Gogglina. And poor Gogglina stared sadly after Golp as he *sproinged* away, getting smaller with each jump.

He disappeared. The frogs said nothing, but crept away one by one, sliding quietly back into the water, until only Gogglina and Grandma Glugga were left.

Gogglina started to cry. "He said I was beautiful …"

"What would he know?" snapped Grandma Glugga. "He's nothing but a low-down wamble-flinker, or I'm a two-headed tadpole! *Men!*"

"I'd never have kissed him if I'd known," said Gogglina miserably.

"Hmm," said Grandma. "That gives me an idea. Wait here!"

She jumped into the pond, and there was a lot of sploshing under the water.

Then Grandma reappeared, wearing her best hat. She only wore her best hat when she meant to *do* something. And when Grandma decided to *do* something, things got *done*.

"Come on," she told Gogglina. "We're going visiting."

"Who are we going to visit?" Gogglina asked.

"A good friend of mine. She's a witch."

"A … witch?" Gogglina gulped nervously. "Is she … wicked?"

"Oho, she is!" said Grandma. "Wily Wanda, the Well Wicked Witch, that's her! I got her crystal ball back for her once, when she tripped over and dropped it in the river, so she owes me a favour."

"Wh-what do you want her to do?" asked Gogglina.

Grandma grinned so widely that Gogglina really thought her head would fall off. "I don't think Golp likes being a frog. I think he'd much rather be a prince again. A pink, hairy, yukky, human prince! And *this* time –"

Gogglina started to grin, too. Poor Golp. No more lovely mud. No more delicious flies. Just cake and peanut butter and ice cream. And princesses. *Gruesome!*

"Yeah!" she said. "This time – no kissy, kissy!"